THE ADVENTURE BEGINS

by Dr. Roy Smith

THE CAMPFIRE GANG BOOK #1

ISBN: 978-1-942292-19-7

Published by Knights of the 21st Century
200 North 7th Street
Lebanon, PA 17046

Copyright © 2017 by Pennsylvania Counseling Services, Inc.

All rights reserved. No part of this book may be reproduced or transmitted in any form or by any means, digital or mechanical, including photocopying, recording, or by any information storage and retrieval system, without the written permission of Pennsylvania Counseling Services, Inc. Requests for permission should be emailed to info@knights21.com.

Knights of the 21st Century is a registered trademark of Pennsylvania Counseling Services, Inc.

Illustrations and book design by Jory Kauffman

Printed in the United States of America

All Scripture quotations are taken from the Holy Bible, New International Reader's Version®, NIrV® Copyright © 1995, 1996, 1998, 2014 by Biblica, Inc.™ Used by permission of Zondervan. All rights reserved worldwide. www.zondervan.com

CONTENTS

1. Bang!   1
2. It's a Long Way Down   12
3. Now What?   30
4. Into the Unknown   46
5. Who's There?   62
6. Building Bridges   78
7. A Time to Fight   97
8. Choosing Your Own Path   113

Dedicated to those who have great value and God-given potential. (This means you!) As you enjoy this series, may you discover your greatness.

I am honored to be part of the journey of the following young men:

Silas

Alexander

Nathan

Mason

William

Lucas

Cody

Elijah

Kent

Colt

Ian

AJ

CJ

JJ

CHAPTER 1

BANG!

The old man's voice echoed into the night. The deep wrinkles on his face flickered in the light of the campfire. A red toothpick hung out of his bearded mouth. It bobbed up and down as he read out loud from a thick, heavy book.

The boys leaned in closer as he talked. Sweat dripped down their faces. Their hearts beat faster and faster. The hero was in trouble… he might not make it! The old man turned the page. Suddenly—

"BANG!"

A loud noise rang out from the woods behind them.

The boys jumped up in a panic. Pete dropped his s'mores on the ground. Kerry tumbled over backward from the log he was sitting on.

The old man stopped reading and waited.

"What was *that*?" BB cried.

Out of the darkness stumbled a slightly round boy. His face turned bright red as he grinned.

"TOBY!" said Pete.

"Are you okay?" BB added. "You smell like burnt popcorn."

"Yeah, I'm fine. They're just fireworks I got from my brother. I wanted to scare you guys a little—that's all."

"Well, you did!" Spencer said.

Pete added, "I don't think that was your best move, Toby. You could've blown yourself up!"

"C'mon, guys!" said Kerry. "We're just getting to the good part." He hated when a good story got interrupted.

Most nights the boys spent their time dreaming up adventures and trips to faraway places. Sometimes they'd play a game they invented. But the nights when the old man came were the best by far.

Toby sat down beside his friends and leaned in. "Keep going, Pops."

Pops, as they called him, always read stories that were jam-packed with heroes, battles and frightening worlds full of terrifying creatures. Tonight was no different.

He waited patiently for the boys to settle down. Then he cleared his throat and continued.

"Roger stared straight into the eyes of the pirate. His leg was bruised, his knuckles were cut, but his will to survive was still alive…"

He paused. "Before I keep going, does anyone know what lesson we can learn here?"

The boys stared at each other. Pops always asked about the lesson behind the story, and each boy would give an answer.

"I think the lesson is that you have to be brave and face your enemies," said Spencer. "That's why he's not backing down."

"I think the lesson is that pirates are always bad guys… no matter how nice they seem," said Pete.

Pops nodded his head in agreement but said nothing. He seemed to be happy when the boys tried to find a meaning in the story and didn't care if their answers were right or wrong.

Then Pops did what he always did after reading to them. He closed his book, got up from his log and quietly said, "See you later."

His red toothpick seemed to glow as he stood up and walked away. The boys watched as he faded into the distance.

"That was a good one," Kerry said.

Everyone nodded in agreement.

"I didn't think Roger was going to make it this time," said Sammy. "He should've listened to Daniel when he told him it was too dangerous to go out to sea."

Cliff nodded. "He was really lucky Daniel came out to help him."

"Of course he came to help him!" said Pete. "That's what friends do. They stick together no matter what."

"Roger was just trying to do what he thought was right," Spencer added.

"Maybe that's the lesson," said Kerry. "Sometimes bad things can happen if you don't listen to someone's advice."

"Or maybe the lesson is that not all ideas are good ideas," BB suggested.

"That makes sense," Cliff agreed.

"Like setting off fireworks!" Toby laughed. "That was probably a bad idea."

Pete added, "If all the bad guys Pops tells us about just blew themselves up like you tried to do, no one would have to be afraid of them."

"It *was* kind of funny," said Cliff. "Remember when Kerry fell off the log?"

Everyone laughed.

"All right, all right." Toby grinned. "It was definitely a bad idea! But at least I'm good at scaring everyone."

"Except Pops," Pete said. "He never seems to be scared of anything. He just sits there and waits."

"Yeah," BB agreed. "It was kind of weird that we all jumped when we heard the bang, but Pops just sat there quietly."

Sammy, who tended to be the quiet one, said, "I saw that too. It seemed like he knew it was going to happen."

"Right!" exclaimed BB. "He didn't move a muscle."

Sammy opened his mouth to say something else, but Kerry jumped in. "Wow! That's pretty cool to think Pops might've known what Toby was going to do."

Toby said, "Well, if that's true, he knows more than me... I usually don't know what I'm going to do until it's over."

They all laughed.

"We all have bad ideas sometimes," said BB. "It can be hard to tell if an idea is good or bad—especially when you're angry."

"If it hurts someone, it's probably a bad idea," said Sammy.

"But what if you hurt someone who's trying to hurt you?" asked Kerry. "Sometimes the kids in Pops' stories have to kill a monster so they don't get eaten."

"I think I'd blow up the monster. I'm pretty good at that," said Toby.

Everyone laughed.

Just then, a strange sound came out of the darkness. It sort of sounded like a sick owl. The boys jumped up. Cupping their hands around their mouths they hooted back into the darkness.

Then a real human voice broke up the hooting party.

"Hey, guys!" A boy walked toward them.

"Where have you been, John?" asked Pete.

"I had to go to my sister's dance competition. It was five hours away. We just got back."

"Dance stuff is the worst," said Spencer. "Jessica does cheerleading. I always hide when it's time to go to her practices."

"I didn't want to go," John said. "But my parents said I had to be a good brother. She always comes to my baseball games, so I guess it's fair."

Kerry laughed. "Oh c'mon, John. You love her and you know it."

"Yeah, I guess I do," John agreed. "I was really proud of her when she did her routine."

"We'd all probably break our necks trying to dance like that," said Pete.

John nodded. "Then we had to take family pictures. I hate that. But she thanked me for coming and that made me feel better. Anyway, what did I miss?"

"Toby almost blew himself up!" said Cliff.

"I think I had what we're calling a bad idea," said Toby. "Take my advice—don't set off a bunch of fireworks at the same time. The bang was so loud I couldn't hear for a while. Now I smell like smoke. But at least I made it out alive!"

"Toby was just trying to scare us," said Kerry. "And it worked! We all just about jumped out of our skin."

John laughed. "I think I'm glad I missed that. How was Pops' story?"

"Roger was almost killed by pirates," BB explained. "But Daniel saved him at the last minute."

"You know," said Pete, "the guys in Pops' stories have bad ideas just like us."

"We do act a lot like them," agreed Kerry.

"They stick together, and so do we," said Spencer. "Even though we're really different from each other, we always stand by each other."

"Let's never stop meeting at the campfire!" shouted Cliff. "Even when we're old like Pops, we'll still come!"

The boys hooted and howled in agreement.

"I told my mom about Pops," Pete admitted. "She said he used to read to her and her friends when they were kids. They loved his stories too."

"I wonder how old he was then," said Toby.

"I don't know," said Pete. "But it sounded like he was just as old then as he is now. She said he had a deep, grumbly voice, a red toothpick and wild beard."

BB stood up and stretched. "It's getting late," he said. "Hey, Sammy, you looked like you wanted to tell us something before. What was it?"

"Well," Sammy said, "I'm not sure what it means, but when I jumped up because of the bang, I saw over Pops' shoulder."

"What's the big deal about that?" Spencer asked. "We all jumped."

Everyone looked at Sammy and waited.

"I saw the pages that Pops was reading from. They were blank. There weren't any words on them."

CHAPTER 2

IT'S A LONG WAY DOWN

BB got up early on Saturday to get his chores over with.

I'll clean the litter box first, he thought, rolling out of bed.

He walked downstairs and took a peek into the box. "Gross!" he said. He glared at the small orange cat sitting on the windowsill. "Boy, do you fill this thing up quick!"

As much as BB loved the cat, cleaning out the litter box really grossed him out. Cleaning up after the dog wasn't quite as bad. At least then he got to be outside and use a much longer shovel.

Next BB headed back to his room. He quickly made his bed and put away the book he was reading the night before.

Unlike most of his friends, his room never got too messy. He liked to keep things neat. Plus his Dad did a room check on Saturday mornings.

The doorbell rang.

"BB!" his mother called. "Sammy's here!"

"Just a second!"

BB ran downstairs. He found his parents and little brother sitting at the kitchen table.

"I'm going fishing with the gang!" he called as he ran past. He grabbed his fishing pole and headed for the door.

Sammy and Kerry were sitting on the front porch, fishing poles in hand.

"Look at the bait my dad gave me," said Kerry. "I'm going to use it to catch The Monster."

Sammy shook his head and turned to BB. "As usual—lots of bragging and no results."

BB laughed.

The Monster was a huge bass that lived in the campground pond down the road. Every once in a while one of the boys would hook him, but he always fought them off and escaped. Toby's stepdad caught him once, but he tossed him back in the water to live another day.

They reached the pond and found John and Pete already hooking bait on their lines. The boys set their gear down in the grass and started to prepare their lines.

"Whoa-whoa-whoaaa!"

They spun around just in time to see Toby fall flat on his face. His pole, net and tackle box flew everywhere.

They howled with laughter.

"I bet he tripped over that muskrat hole," Pete said.

"Your front flip is almost as good as my sister's!" John chuckled.

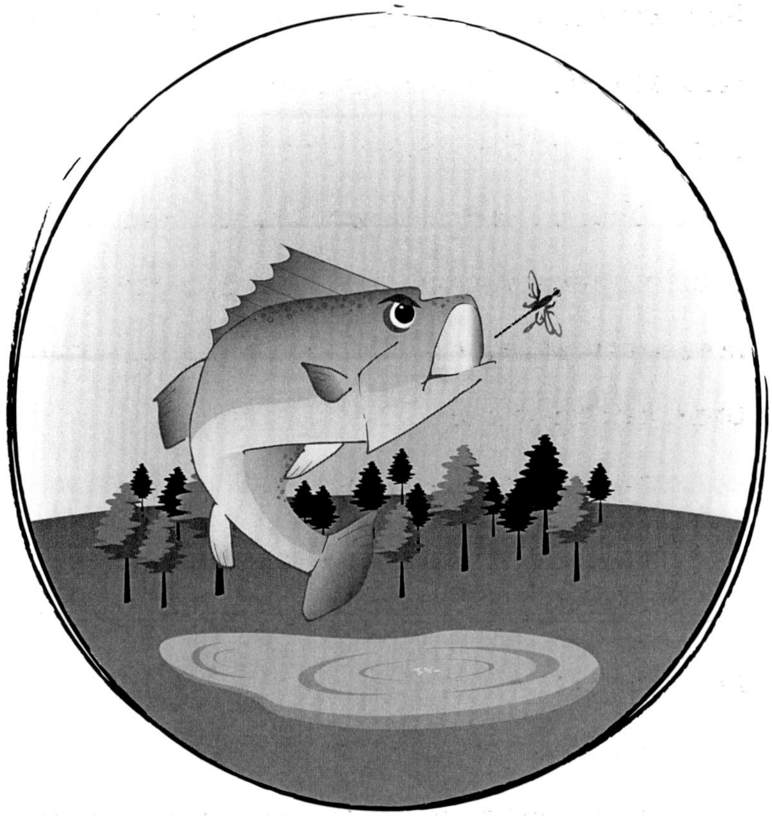

They helped Toby collect his gear and started fishing. The boys caught sunnies, catfish and a couple of small bass. Whoever caught the most fish had bragging rights until the next time. The Monster teased Kerry by jumping up in front of him twice.

As always, the boys threw their fish right back into the water so they could have the fun of catching them another day.

Just as they were about to leave, the sound of owl hoots echoed frantically from the trees next to the campground. The boys hooted back.

Cliff and Spencer darted out of the forest.

"Where have you been?" BB asked. "You missed a great day of fishing!"

"We jumped the fence at the old quarry," Spencer answered, struggling to catch his breath.

"You did what?!" cried John.

"Cliff talked me into it!"

Pete's eyes widened. "Are you crazy? Haven't you heard the stories about people disappearing there?"

"I heard that a whole football team vanished when their bus slipped off the road and went straight through the fence," Toby added.

"Yeah, I've heard it all," Cliff said. "But we still wanted to see what was in there."

"My stepdad said if you fall in one of those holes you'll never get out," said Toby. "It's a maze—there are hundreds of miles of tunnels down there. He's a geologist. His job is to study rocks. He said the quarry used to be one of the richest silver mines ever. But they built too many tunnels in such a small area that it made the ground too weak to mine anymore."

Pete turned excitedly to Spencer and Cliff. "What was it like?"

"Well," Spencer began, "it was kind of scary at first. But once we got inside the fence and started exploring, it was really cool."

"Come see for yourself!" Cliff called as he ran back toward the woods.

The others looked at each other nervously.

"I don't know..." BB said. "It seems dangerous."

"Scaredy-cats!" Pete called as he ran after Cliff.

One by one the boys followed after Cliff and Pete.

The fence surrounding the quarry seemed to stretch on for miles. A giant DO NOT ENTER sign hung on the side facing the boys. They gathered close to it and peered through the fence.

Spencer pressed his face into the chain link as if trying to break through. "I wish we could see what's in those tunnels," he sighed.

"If there's still silver in there, we could be rich!" said Cliff.

"Maybe the ghosts of those football players

are in there!" said Toby.

Everyone except Kerry, BB and Sammy set down their fishing gear and climbed over. The three boys decided to stay outside the fence and be the lookouts.

As the guys walked further into the quarry, Spencer leaned toward Cliff.

"Should we show them?" he whispered.

"I don't know—should we?"

Toby suddenly popped up beside them. "Show us what?" he asked suspiciously.

Cliff smiled. "C'mon, follow me!"

They made a right and crossed several mining roads.

Cliff finally stopped. "There," he said.

He pointed at a dirt-covered school bus sitting beside a giant sinkhole.

"Whoa..." they all whispered.

"Is... is that the bus that the football players disappeared in?" Toby asked.

"Maybe there are ghosts in there!" shouted John.

"Maybe there are skeletons!" exclaimed Pete.

"You know, there's only one way to find out," Cliff said with a mischievous grin.

Spencer reached the door first. He slowly pulled it open. It let out a loud creak.

"There's nothing but dirt in here," Toby said, covering his mouth to cough.

Everyone but John stepped inside. He walked toward the sinkhole and stood at the edge.

"This thing is huge!" he yelled. "I can't see the bottom at all. I think we better—"

Suddenly the bus shifted downward. Dirt and rocks and a giant boulder poured down against the front door.

Spencer ran to the back door of the bus. "Both doors are jammed!"

"I think we're trapped!" Toby yelled out a window.

"Let me get the other guys to help," John said. "The four of us should be able to pull it open together."

"Okay," Pete said. "But don't forget where we are. This quarry is awfully big, and it's getting dark."

John ran back toward the fence. "Guys!" he yelled.

"Over here!" Kerry called.

John ran toward the other boys and stopped to catch his breath.

"What happened?" BB asked. "Where's everyone else?"

"They're stuck in an old school bus. Somehow the ground shifted and a big boulder rammed against the door. We need your help."

"You look like a mess," said Sammy.

"I took a shortcut through the swamp. I fell a couple times and hit some jagger bushes."

He held out one arm so they could see the bright red scrapes across it.

"Do you remember how to get back to the bus?" Kerry asked.

"Yeah," said John. "But we're going to have to take a longer way. I don't want to go through that swamp again."

"Good idea," said Kerry. He climbed over the fence, and Sammy and BB quickly followed.

"Here it is," John said when they finally got to the bus. The others looked out the bus windows and cheered as the four boys ran toward them. They pushed and pulled on the big rusty door. But it refused to open.

"Hold on," BB said. "This isn't working. It's just making us tired."

"I have an idea!" Kerry said. "When I say *one*, you guys inside the bus all run to one side of the bus. When I say *two*, run to the other side. Maybe that will rock the bus away from the boulder."

Everyone agreed that Kerry's idea might work. As they rocked the bus back and forth, BB shoved a stick between the boulder and the door. The next time, John shoved another stick in.

Just when the plan seemed to be working, there was a thunderous "THUMP." The bus, everyone inside and the four boys holding onto sticks outside of it disappeared into the huge sinkhole.

The bus came crashing to a stop and the door flew open. Kerry, BB, Sammy and John quickly scrambled inside. They made it in just in time.

As soon as they sat down beside the others, the big boulder that was leaning against the bus came crashing down on top of the opening they had just jumped into.

"Oh no," BB groaned. "Now we're *really* trapped."

"What are we going to do *now*?" Pete cried.

"Is everyone okay?" Sammy asked into the darkness.

"I'm okay," Kerry answered. "I just have a couple of scratches. That rock was way too close to crushing us."

"Wow," said John. "It felt like we fell a long way down. I really bumped my head, but I think I'm okay."

"Anyone have a flashlight?" Spencer asked hopefully.

"No," the boys replied.

"How are we going to get out of here?" Toby asked. "We can't go back out through that door."

Pete said. "If we can't get ourselves out, who's going to find us way down here?"

"We left our gear outside the fence," BB

reminded them. "When someone comes looking for us, maybe they'll see our gear and come inside the fence to find us. Cliff, why don't you and Spencer try to feel your way to the front of the bus? Check under the driver's seat for tools, fire extinguishers or anything you can find. The rest of us better sit down and try to relax. The last thing we want to do is rock this bus again. It might drop even further."

The group was quiet as Cliff and Spencer felt their way to the front of the bus.

Sammy said, "We always feel good when Pops reads to us and asks us questions. Since he's not here, I'll ask for him—what's the lesson we can learn here?"

"I learned that when there's a sign on a fence that says DO NOT ENTER, maybe I should listen," said Kerry.

Everyone nodded their heads in the dark.

John said, "I learned that it's not smart to

rock a bus when it's sitting on weak ground."

"I learned that Kerry stinks at fishing," Pete smiled. "I wish I was back at the pond right now watching The Monster mess with him."

"BB," Toby said, "you're good at figuring out the lessons we need to learn. What do you think?"

"Well, I have an idea, but I don't want you all to get mad at me. We have to keep working together as a team."

"C'mon, BB," said Toby. "We're strong enough to take it."

"Well," BB began, "the lesson I learned was about pressure from my friends. I knew I shouldn't jump the fence. I thought about the lesson we learned when Toby almost blew himself up. We decided that some ideas aren't good. But instead of standing up for what I thought I should do, I went along with a bad idea. Sometimes we know we shouldn't do something, but when others want to do it, we do it anyway. I needed to be strong and do what I thought was right."

"I think you're right," Pete said. Everyone else agreed.

By this time Spencer and Cliff had made their way back to the gang.

"Spencer found a toolbox," Cliff said. "It's got a hammer, a few screwdrivers, a crowbar, some other small tools and a bunch of clips. I found a tow chain, a long rope, a can of WD-40 and a first-aid kit."

Spencer added, "We also found a fire extinguisher. And you'll never guess what we found in the glove box."

"What?" Toby said impatiently. "Tell us!"

Spencer pulled something bright out of his back pocket. "You know those red toothpicks Pops keeps in his mouth? The ones that look like they're glowing? I found a whole box of them. Look at all the light they give off!"

"Wow," said John. "That's great! We'll be able to use them tonight. I think we're going to have to sleep here."

"I think you're right," Pete agreed. "But how did Pops' toothpicks get here?"

BB was deep in thought. "There's something strange about Pops. It seems like he was really old even when our parents were young. He reads out of a book that doesn't have any words in it. He knew Toby's fireworks were going to go off before they did. And now this—his toothpicks actually glow."

"We needed light, and here it is," Sammy said.

The gang grew quiet. They were each thinking about Pops.

"I wonder if he knew we'd be here," Toby said out loud to himself.

Each boy asked himself the same question as they tried to fall asleep.

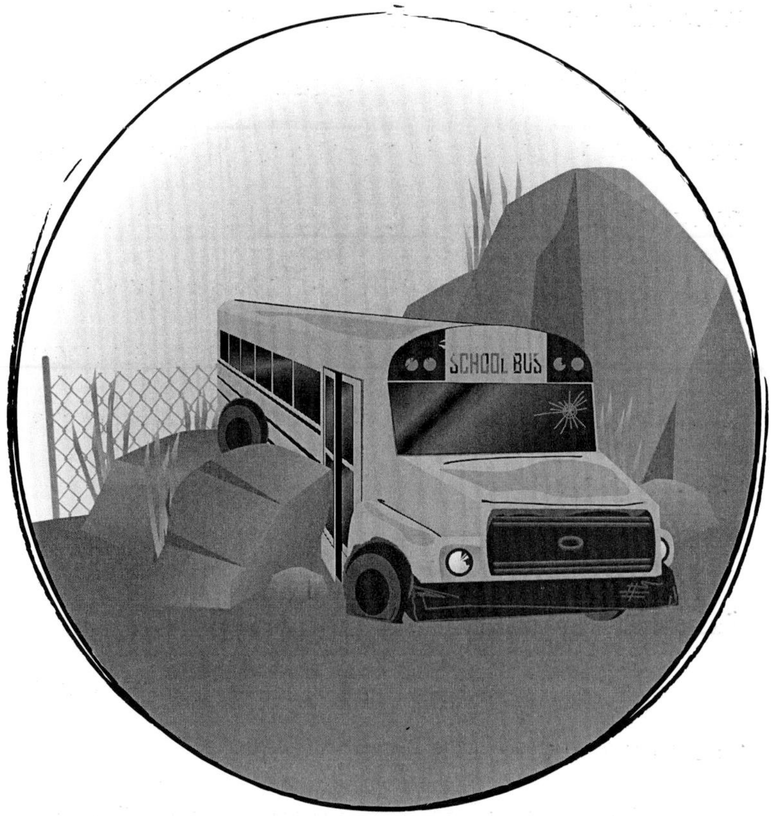
SCHOOL BUS

CHAPTER 3

NOW WHAT?

The bus was quiet and dark. Spencer had covered up the glowing toothpicks so the gang could try to get some sleep.

After what seemed like hours Spencer was still wide awake. He finally whispered, "Are any of you guys awake?"

"I am!" each boy answered.

"I wonder what time it is," Pete said.

John answered, "I have no idea."

"How long have we been down here?" Kerry asked.

"Too long," said John. "I'm getting really hungry. I wonder how long it's going to take for us to get out of here."

"We don't know how far this bus went down into the hole," Cliff said. "And if you look up you can't see any light coming from above. This has got to be a really deep sinkhole."

"Sounds like we're stuck pretty good," Sammy said. He took a deep breath and added, "I'm scared."

"It's okay to be scared," said Toby, trying to be brave. "I think we all are. But now we have to decide what to do about it."

"Yeah," Cliff agreed. "Sitting here and waiting isn't the answer."

"Remember the lesson we learned from one of Pops' stories?" BB asked. "We talked about how a bad plan is better than no plan at all."

"I remember that one," Kerry said. "We talked about how we have to face our fears and try to beat them. That's better than not trying at all."

"Even if what you do doesn't work," BB added. "Then you'll at least learn from your mistakes. And you can always try something different the next time."

Kerry said, "I remember wondering why so many bad things happen in the world. So many people are sitting around doing nothing. If we work together we could try to stop the bad things. Like people getting sick, fighting or starving."

"I hear a lot of grownups complaining about how hard life is," Spencer said. "But it doesn't seem like they're trying to fix it. It's like they want someone else to do the hard work for them."

"All of that makes sense," said Sammy. "So what you're saying is we need a plan. We can't just wait for someone to save us."

"But what if our plan doesn't work?" John asked nervously. "We could be stuck in here forever."

"Let's not talk about that," BB said calmly. "It only makes us more scared. Then we won't have the courage to do anything to fix it. Let's come up with a plan that could make things better. Why don't we make a list of things that are important for us to do?"

"We should try to only move around when we need to," Cliff said. "We don't know what the bus is sitting on. If we rock it again it could crash down deeper."

"Okay," Kerry agreed. "Rule number one—no one moves around until we decide what we're doing."

Pete said, "I think we should test out how strong the light is from one of Pops' toothpicks. We might be able to take them out of the box. Then more than one of us can have a light."

"Sounds good," said John. "That's rule number two—we each get a few toothpick lights to keep with us."

Spencer looked around. "I think we can agree that we're all afraid of never getting out of here. So I think we shouldn't talk about how scared we are. We should only talk about our plan."

"You're right," Toby said. "I feel like crying. But that's not going to help get us out of here. Let's make that rule number three—no complaining or talking about what we're afraid of. Focus on the plan."

"Does everyone agree with these rules?" BB asked.

"Yes!" everyone said at once.

"Any other rules we should have?"

"Yeah," John said. "I think if we get out of this bus we should all stick together. We need all of our muscle and brain power to figure this out. I don't want to leave anyone behind."

"I don't want to go anywhere without you guys either," Kerry said. "That should be rule number four—stick together unless there's a really good reason not to."

"I got us into this mess by climbing over the fence in the first place," Cliff said. "Now I want to help get us out. But first I think we need a leader. BB was right that we shouldn't have started exploring the quarry. So I think he should be our leader."

"I agree," Pete said. "We need a leader to organize us. And he can run the meetings we'll need to have to figure out how to get out of here."

Toby called out, "Everyone in favor of BB, say 'aye!'"

"Aye!" echoed loudly through the bus.

"Okay," said BB. "But if you want me to agree to be the leader, we need another rule. We all have to vote on the big things. Everyone always needs to say their ideas out loud. No one should hold anything back. Even if we don't use your idea, we all need to work together. So rule number five—support the group's decisions even when you don't get your way."

Everyone agreed.

Spencer spoke up. "I have a rule—but it's just for you, Cliff. You can't keep thinking this was all your fault. We all made this mistake together, and we're going to get out of it together. You need to forgive yourself and let it go."

"Yeah," John agreed. "We're all in this together. I vote Cliff lets it go and joins our team!"

"All in favor?" BB called.

"Aye!" everyone yelled back.

"Thanks, guys," Cliff said with tears in his eyes.

BB put his hand on Cliff's shoulder. "Now," he said, "Spencer and Cliff found some tools we can use. Let's do something my dad calls brainstorming, where we talk about everyone's ideas.

We have to think through all the ideas we have, so keep coming up with new ones. Brainstorming helps us come up with something we might've never thought of on our own. It's going to take some pretty amazing ideas to get us out of here."

"Well," Spencer piped up, "we could spray WD-40 on the boulder and try to slide the bus off of it."

Pete said, "We could break a window to climb out of. Then we could climb on top of the boulder and try to see the opening at the top of this pit."

"If there's gas in the bus tank," Toby said, "I could spread it on the boulder and light it. That might make a bang that a search party could hear and use to find us."

Cliff laughed. "I'm worried about you, Toby. You seem to like fire and loud noises a little too much."

Toby smiled. "Can you blame me?"

Spencer's voice cut through the laughter. "We keep trying to go up..." he said slowly. "But what if we try to go down instead?"

"What do you mean?" BB asked.

"Well, remember that giant hurricane a couple years ago? After it happened the creeks were all overflowing. I decided to explore the creek bed behind my house to see if anything cool washed up. But the rocks around the creek were so slippery that I fell right into the water. Then I got sucked into a whirlpool. I really thought I was going to drown. When I tried to swim above the water it just kept pulling me back into the whirlpool. But then I tried to swim straight down underwater. When I did that, the water couldn't pull me as hard. I finally made it back to the bank and climbed out."

"I see what you're saying," Sammy said. "We know this sinkhole's really deep. Instead of wasting our energy trying to go back the way we came, we could try to find another way out."

"The tunnels!" Toby said excitedly. "Remember the ones my stepdad told me about? They have to lead above ground somewhere. If we can make it to the tunnels we could try to find our way out."

"Maybe there are signs in the tunnels," Pete said. "You know, like directions so the miners wouldn't get lost."

"There might be tracks too," John added, "that they used for the mine cars to carry the silver out. If we find one of those it'll lead us back outside."

"That's true," BB said. "But sometimes they pull all of those old tracks out when they close up a mine. Either way it's worth a shot."

The gang talked about this new idea for what seemed like hours. Finally everyone agreed to try to pry open the back door of the bus and head downward.

Everyone stood still and tried not to rock the bus. Kerry slowly sprayed some WD-40 around the edges of the back door. Then Pete stuck the crowbar through the side. He and John pulled as hard as they could.

After a lot of tugging, the door flew open and banged against something. Kerry took some glowing toothpicks and leaned outside.

"There's a wall right beside us," he said as he leaned back inside the bus. "But I can't see the ground at all. I think there's a drop-off right behind the bus."

Pete and John pulled the door closed again and sat down inside the bus.

"I think we need a new plan," Sammy said quietly.

"When Pops taught us that we need to have a plan," BB said, "we also learned that no plan is perfect. You always have to be ready to make adjustments."

"I remember talking about that," Sammy said. "We realized that we always have to try really hard when we want to do anything important. Getting through a problem is never easy."

"And when you finally get through it," John added, "it makes you stronger. The harder you work for something, the better you feel when you finally get it."

Spencer nodded. "That's how getting out of here will be. Our first plan failed, but we still need to keep trying."

"Cliff found this tow chain," Toby said. "I think one of us should go out the back hooked onto the chain to see how deep the drop-off is."

"I'll do it!" Spencer said quickly. "I weigh the least and I used to take gymnastics. Plus we'll need you bigger guys to pull me back in."

BB looked around. "What do the rest of you think about this plan?"

"It's risky," Pete said. "But I think it's better than staying here."

"Cliff and Spencer found those steel clips too," John added. "We could clip one end of the chain around Spencer and the other to the front of the bus. That would help keep Spencer safe."

"Good idea," Kerry said. "It could save Spencer if the chain slips out of our hands."

Toby said, "We'll all hold on really tight. We won't drop you, Spencer."

"Has everyone said everything they want to?" BB asked.

"Yes!" everyone answered.

"Spencer, are you sure you want to try this?"

"Yes. I'm actually pretty good at this kind of thing. Plus, when I'm scared, I move like a monkey. So I'm ready to go!" Spencer blew his cheeks out and howled like a monkey.

The guys all laughed. Then they began to plan how to lower Spencer from the bus and how to pull him back up. They moved around the bus slowly to make sure they didn't rock it.

Kerry clipped the chain onto a pole behind the driver's seat. Then each boy slowly spread out in a line. Toby stood closest to the back door, followed by Cliff.

John hooked the other end of the chain to Spencer. Pete used a Band-Aid from the first-aid kit to tape some glowing toothpicks onto Spencer's head like a miner's hat.

Everyone worked quietly on their tasks. They all thought about Spencer and what would happen next. So far nothing was going as expected.

When everything was ready, each boy stood silently in his place wondering, *Will this plan work or just make things worse?*

Sammy broke the silence first. "Guys," he began, "you know I go to church. My dad's a pastor. I know some of you believe in God and some of you probably don't. But before we open the door and Spencer goes out into the unknown, is it okay if I pray for all of us?"

"I'd feel better if we did that," Kerry said.

"Me too," Spencer agreed. "I need to stay strong. And I also need to think clearly so I can remember what I see down there."

"What do you all think?" BB asked. "We're in this together."

Everyone agreed that Sammy should pray. The bus was silent again.

Sammy closed his eyes. "God, you're like our father and we sure need one now. Help us take care of Spencer. I know you love him and want everything to be okay for him. Help us do the right thing. And thanks for taking care of us so far in this mess. Show Spencer a way to get us all out of here. Amen."

Everyone looked at Spencer. Something had changed about him. The red toothpicks that were taped to his head seemed to be glowing brighter than ever.

Without saying anything, Toby and Cliff opened the door. They grabbed the chain firmly.

Spencer looked at each of his friends. "See you later," he said—and he slid out into the darkness.

CHAPTER 4

INTO THE UNKNOWN

The chain swung gently back and forth as the gang slowly lowered Spencer down into the darkness.

This is nothing like gymnastics practice, Spencer thought to himself. He tried not to think about the deep, dark empty space that stretched out below him.

This was one of the times Spencer wished he was older than he was—like when his grandmother had died suddenly. His mom cried for a week. He had tried to help out more with his younger sisters. He felt like a grownup when he poured them cereal or helped put them to bed.

Spencer knew he had to act like a grownup to do this dangerous task.

He looked up and saw Toby's hand holding onto the chain at the back of the bus.

"I'm not going to let them down," Spencer said quietly.

He thought about how much he trusted them to hold on to that chain. He knew they trusted him just as much to stay calm and look for a way out.

If I weren't hanging over a giant pit, Spencer thought, *this would actually be really fun.*

Spencer had always loved climbing, swimming and playing sports—even if he was usually the smallest kid on the field.

As the gang lowered him slowly, he looked around. The light coming off of his toothpicks made the walls look smooth and bright.

Spencer didn't understand how Pops' toothpicks glowed like they did. But he sure was glad to have a batch of them taped to his head.

Suddenly he found himself hanging in front of two large tunnels carved into the wall of the drop-off. He looked down. The ground was still nowhere to be seen.

To reach the tunnels Spencer would have to swing back and forth. If he swung hard enough, he might be able to catch the edge of one of them.

Spencer gave a loud hoot. The gang stopped lowering him.

"You okay?" Toby called.

"Yeah!"

Spencer started to swing his legs back and forth—like he was on a swing set. Pretty soon his whole body was swinging toward one of the tunnels.

He reached out to try to grab the edge of the tunnel. His fingertips brushed it, but he wasn't able to get a good grip. A pebble fell into the darkness below him.

Plunk! The pebble hit something.

He looked down again as he swung. This time he could make out a shadow of something below him.

It looked like a bridge.

Suddenly Spencer felt the chain jerk a bit.

"We're out of chain!" Toby called. "We're going to bring you back up!"

The way back up seemed to take much longer than the way down. When Spencer finally climbed into the bus again everyone cheered. They high-fived and hugged each other.

Spencer sat down and let out a big "whew!" Everyone started talking and asking questions all at once.

"Give him some air!" BB said loudly. "Tell us everything you saw, Spencer."

"First I want to say thanks," Spencer said. "You guys took care of me. You didn't let go. And then you pulled me the whole way back up."

Spencer explained what the walls of the drop-off looked like and about the two tunnels and bridge.

"The toothpicks helped me see almost everything around me," he said. "It made me feel like Pops was right there with me."

BB asked Spencer what he thought they should do.

"We'd have to swing ourselves to the tunnels. I don't know if everyone can swing hard enough," he said. "We'd probably need to swing four to five feet to catch the edge."

"That sounds kind of dangerous," said Kerry. "What if we fall?"

"You'd hit the bridge pretty hard. And you'd fall even further if you missed it."

"Is there another way to the tunnels?" Pete asked.

Spencer nodded. "I could unhook myself from the chain when I get to the end of it. Then I can jump down a couple feet onto the bridge and walk across it to get to one of the tunnels."

He stopped for a second, deep in thought. Then he continued. "You know, when I was down there I think I heard running water. It sounded like it was coming from the tunnel on my left."

"I'm really thirsty," Cliff groaned.

"Me too!"

"I'm hungry!"

"So am I!"

"Guys," BB interrupted, "we can't panic. We've got to figure out what to do next."

"We could stay here for a couple days and see if someone finds us," Pete suggested.

"With no food or water—yeah right!" Cliff said. "We've got to find that water."

"I don't know if we could swing the chain far enough to catch the edge of the tunnel," Spencer said. "With so many of us, someone's bound to fall. Hitting the bridge would hurt. And missing the bridge altogether would be even worse."

"Plus we might rock the bus if we're all trying to swing the chain," Kerry added. "I don't want to pull the bus down on top of us."

"Yeah," Sammy agreed. "I think the best option would be to jump those few feet onto the bridge and hope it holds us."

"We're going to have to be brave enough to unhook ourselves for that last step," John said. "I'll feel safer being hooked to the chain."

Sammy nodded. "We're all going to have to make that jump—even though we're not sure what will happen."

The boys all agreed that this plan made them nervous.

"This is risky," BB said. "But I think jumping onto the bridge is our only option. It reminds me of another lesson Pops taught us. We keep saying we're all in this together. But Pops taught us there are times when you feel like no one is there to help you. Those are the times when you need to do things on your own because you know it's the right thing to do."

BB looked around at all his friends. "When we get lowered into that pit we're going to feel pretty alone. It'll be dark and scary. Just remember that we're all in this together. Even when you can't see us, we're rooting for you."

Spencer nodded. "That's what I did and it helped a lot."

"I'm glad we made you the leader, BB," Cliff said. "I was there for most of Pops' stories. But I can't always remember the lessons."

Kerry added, "And you're good at using the lessons in real life."

"Thanks, guys," BB said. "I'm good at remembering stuff like that. Now let's make a plan!"

They decided to lower Kerry first since he was tall and thin and could carry the bag of tools down with him. He could also reach up and hopefully help the others jump onto the bridge safely.

Toby and Cliff would go next because they were heavy. They would need everyone's help to hold all of their weight.

Then the rest of the gang would follow—with BB and Spencer at the very end. Spencer said he could go down the chain without help. He had learned a special grip at gymnastics practice.

Kerry hooked himself to the chain.

"Wait," he said. "Before we do this—Sammy, will you pray again?"

Everyone agreed, and Sammy closed his eyes.

"God," he began, "we're pretty scared. Please keep us safe as we try to get to the bridge.

Please be with Spencer as he climbs down all by himself. And help us figure out a way to get out of here. Amen."

Kerry held on to the chain and worked his way down. After a while they heard him hoot. He had landed safely on the bridge. Toby followed, then Cliff, Pete, Sammy, John, BB and finally Spencer.

As Spencer let go of the chain and dropped safely below, the boys looked around in amazement. They couldn't believe they had all made it!

"Wow," John whispered as he looked up. "I can barely see the bus up there." It seemed far away.

BB turned to Spencer. "Which way's the water?"

"That way, I think."

"We should stick together," BB said. "All in favor of trying this tunnel first?"

"Aye!"

Cliff took the lead. Each boy had a few glowing toothpicks taped to his head with a Band-Aid. They were so bright it almost looked like daytime.

The sound of running water got louder and louder as the boys walked downhill through the tunnel.

Eventually they found themselves in a small, cave-like room. The lights from their toothpicks glistened off of a giant pool of water in the middle of the cave.

"Do you think it's safe to drink?" Cliff asked, looking cautiously at the water.

"It looks clean," Toby said, leaning down to try it.

He smacked his lips together. "Tastes like sulfur. Sometimes ours tastes like this at home. But my stepdad always says it's okay to drink."

The boys immediately cupped their hands and began to slurp.

Just when they had drank as much as they could, a giant "CRACK" made them jump.

"BANG! BANG! BANG!" they heard.

They ran back to the entrance of the tunnel. The bus was gone!

They looked down just in time to see the bus and the bridge disappear into the darkness below.

The tow chain and the pole it was hooked onto were stuck like a spear in the tunnel entrance.

Toby quickly unhooked the chain and handed the pole to Cliff. "We might need these later on," he said.

"I guess we got out of there just in time," John said.

The boys walked slowly and silently back to the cave room. Each boy was lost in his own thoughts.

Finally Sammy broke the silence. "Thank you, God," he prayed. "You helped us get out of that bus at just the right time. Amen."

BB took a deep breath. "We always have a lot of fun together. It's easy for us to pretend everything's fun and games. But sometimes serious things like this happen. We could've died just now. Pretending everything's a game can get us in trouble. Like when we climbed the quarry fence and got into that bus. Or when Toby almost set himself on fire."

Toby smiled.

"We all worked hard together," BB continued. "That's why we're still here. We'll get through this by sticking together and helping each other. And we've got to remember some of Pops' lessons and keep learning more lessons. Now let's look around and see what else we can find in this cave."

After a few minutes of searching, the boys heard Toby yell. "Guys!" he called. "Check this out."

He pointed toward the ceiling of the cave. Three huge fossils stuck out from the wall.

"I wish I would've listened to my stepdad more," Toby said. "He knows all about fossils. I usually just pretend to listen."

"Let's keep going down the tunnel and see if we can find another way out of here," Pete said.

After walking for a few minutes, Toby suddenly tripped over a rock and fell head-first onto the ground. Cliff, who was right behind him, tripped over Toby and fell beside him.

A loud groan sounded as Toby and Cliff picked themselves up.

"Are you okay?" Pete asked.

They both nodded.

"Did you make that sound?" BB asked.

"What sound?"

"Somebody definitely groaned."

"Maybe it was just the rocks tapping against each other," Kerry suggested.

"No," BB insisted. "It was a groan. Where did it come from?"

They spread out to look.

BB looked around the rock Toby and Cliff had tripped over. He stepped on top of it as he went to walk by. They heard another loud groan.

Everyone froze and looked at BB.

"That rock groaned," John said. "I know rocks don't do that. But I'm telling you—it did."

They all took turns briefly stepping on the rock. Each time a loud groan bellowed out.

Then they tried stepping on other rocks. Nothing happened.

"Maybe we should bring it back to the cave," Spencer said. "Then we can look at it closer. Plus, I'm getting tired."

They all agreed.

Just as they were spreading out on the ground to sleep, Pete shouted, "Hey, guys!"

"What?"

Pete pointed to the ceiling. "Those giant fossils Toby saw earlier... they're gone!"

CHAPTER 5

WHO'S THERE?

The gang didn't know what time they woke up the next day, but at some point they all got up and started exploring.

Several boys walked back toward the bridge to see if it was still gone. It was. Others searched all over the cave walls to see if they could find the missing fossils.

BB and Sammy kept poking and turning over the rock. Every time they stood on it, it let out a loud groan.

They learned something new about the rock too—if they stood on it long enough it would vibrate a little.

Sammy was the first to discover this. He jumped off as soon as it began to shake.

"That's not good," he said. "What if it's an old bomb the miners used to dig out these tunnels?"

The boys stared at the rock nervously. The vibrating stopped.

Pete came over and poked it. "Look at this," he said. He pointed to some markings on the underside of the rock.

"It sort of looks like somebody wrote on it," BB said.

Toby walked over to them.

"What's going on?" he asked.

They showed him the markings. He took a step back and rubbed his chin.

"That's funny," he said. "From here it looks like a drawing of Pops' face. It's got his beard and everything."

The boys looked closer.

"You're right!" BB said. "Hey, guys," he called to the rest of the boys. "You've got to see this."

They dropped what they were doing and ran over.

"Look at these markings. Don't they look like Pops' face with his wild beard? This line here could even be his toothpick."

"It does look like him," John agreed.

"Everything we find always seems to lead us back to Pops," Kerry said. "I wonder if he's been here before. If we could find him, we could ask him to help us."

"If only we found a magic rock," Cliff said. "All this rock's good for is groaning."

"Well, that's not exactly true," BB said. "We just found out it also vibrates if you stand on it long enough."

Sammy added, "It almost feels like it's going to explode. I was afraid it might be a bomb so I got off."

"Let me try," Cliff said.

Everyone stood back as Cliff stepped onto the rock. Suddenly it groaned loudly. Then it began to vibrate.

"See, we told you," said Sammy.

It shook harder and harder. Cliff was about to jump off when a loud voice said,

"Everyone who has this kind of knowledge will be given more knowledge. In fact, they will have very much. If anyone doesn't have this kind of knowledge, even what little they have will be taken away from them." *

The gang froze in stunned silence. Cliff's eyes looked like they might pop out of his head.

---

*   Matthew 13:12

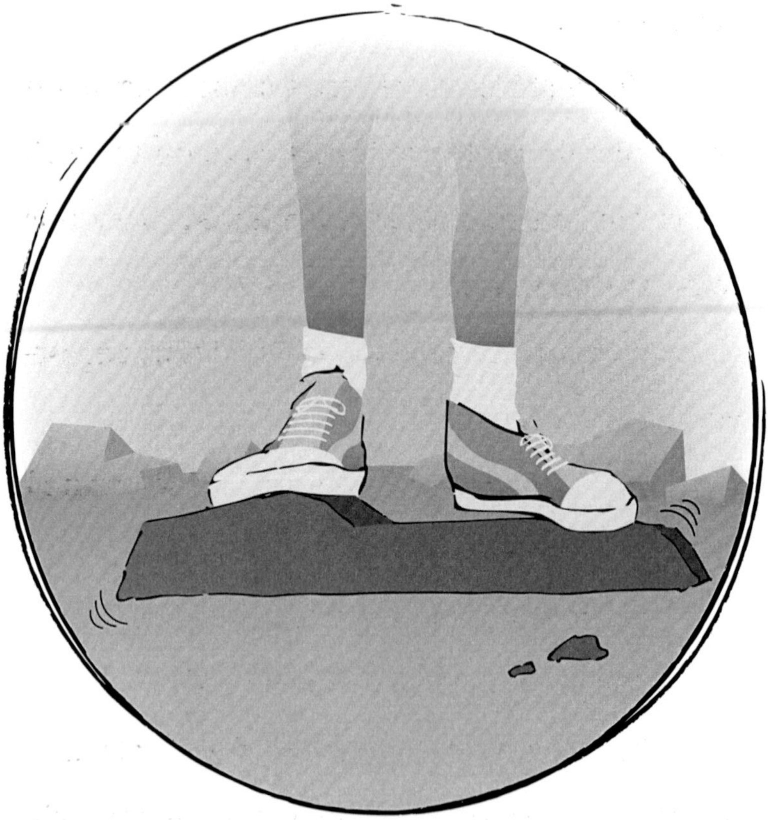

"Did you hear that?" he asked. "Or was it my imagination?"

"We heard it," Toby said.

"It sounded like it came from the rock," Sammy said.

Kerry shivered. "There's something weird about this place. Those fossils were on the wall yesterday and then they disappeared. Now this rock is talking to us."

"Let's see if it'll do it again," John suggested. "I'll try this time."

John stepped onto the rock. They waited quietly. No groan, no vibration, no voice.

"Maybe it's mad at us," Sammy said.

"Maybe it died," Cliff suggested.

"We keep talking about *why* it talked..." Spencer pointed out. "But maybe we should talk about *what* it said. If Pops were here he'd say, 'What's the lesson we can learn here?'"

"It said something about 'everyone who knows something will get more,'" BB said. "Maybe the rock was telling us to listen to it and do what it says."

Sammy nodded. "It's like a Bible verse my dad preached about once. He said if you learn something good and use it to help you do what's right, then God will help you learn even more. But if you don't do it, God won't teach you new things."

"I knew it wasn't right to climb over the fence, but I did it anyway," BB said. "And now we're stuck here."

"When I tried to get the rock to talk without really listening first, it got quiet," John pointed out.

The toothpicks on the boys' heads began to glow even brighter.

"I think we should bring the rock along with us. It might have something else to teach us," Pete said.

"Good idea," BB said. "Now let's get going. We can take turns being the leader."

"I'll go first," Toby volunteered.

They headed down the tunnel and away from the cave. Every now and then they stopped for a rest, but because they were in a hurry they never stopped for long.

Spencer, who was at the back of the line, began to feel strange. He glanced behind him and then poked John.

"I think someone's following us," he whispered.

They decided to quickly duck around the next corner. Covering up their lights with their shirts, they waited for whatever was following them.

It only took a few seconds for them to see the outlines of three forms speeding quietly by them.

John immediately uncovered his light while Spencer yelled, "Watch out! Get them!"

Spencer and John ran after whatever was following them. The other boys doubled back to help. But when they met each other in the middle, the creatures were gone.

"Did you see them?" John asked.

"See who?" Kerry answered, looking confused.

Spencer and John explained everything. The boys decided to spread out to find whatever was following them.

Pete put the talking rock down. Then, on a whim, he stood on it.

A loud groan echoed through the tunnel. Pete felt the rock vibrate and everyone heard a voice say,

"So we don't spend all our time looking at what we can see. Instead, we look at what we can't see. That's because what can be seen lasts only a short time. But what can't be seen will last forever." *

"Well," Toby said, "I think we can all agree now. That definitely came out of the rock."

"It doesn't make sense," Cliff said. "How can we look at something we can't see?"

"Remember how we decided that some ideas are good and some are bad?" BB said. "Sometimes it's hard to see why an idea's good or bad. Like when your parents tell you that eating broccoli is good for you. It tastes gross and looks weird so you'd think it would be bad. But there's something you can't see or taste that makes it good. So that's the part of the broccoli you have to focus on, even though it's invisible."

"Huh?" said Toby, looking puzzled.

---

* 2 Corinthians 4:18

"I think I get it," Kerry said. "While we're trying to get out of here we should pay attention to what's not easy to see or understand. That might help us more than just doing what we're comfortable with."

"Oh."

"You sound like my dad," Sammy said. "Pastors always say things like that."

"John and Spencer said they felt something following them but then it disappeared," Cliff said. "Maybe that's it. Let's see if we can find it again."

They split up into two-person search parties and got to work.

Kerry and Toby searched along one of the tunnel walls.

"Toby, come here," Kerry said. He reached up and grabbed ahold of a fossil sticking out of the wall. "This looks just like the fossils we found in the cave."

Suddenly the fossil started to wiggle and squirm in Kerry's hand.

"It's alive!" he yelled.

Two big legs sprouted out from its back and a bunch of smaller legs lined its stomach. It looked like it could either run upright or flatten out like a giant bug.

Toby ran up and grabbed its legs. Kerry took off his belt, wrapped it around the wriggling creature and fastened it tightly.

It was the weirdest looking thing they'd ever seen. It looked a lot taller than Toby, but it was thin and seemed to be pretty weak.

"Let me go! Let *me* go!" the creature shouted.

By this time the rest of the gang had heard the commotion and came rushing over. They surrounded the creature like a pack of wolves, ready to fight if they needed to.

The boys all looked at the creature. It looked back at them. Its large eyes looked nervous and angry.

"Let him go. He's our brother," a high-pitched voice squeaked out of the darkness.

The boys spun around. Two similar-looking creatures walked toward them on their back legs.

"Who are you?" BB called out. "And why are you following us?"

"My name is Jepson," one growled. He had scaly and yellowish skin. "We belong to the Clamps. This is our home. We haven't had a human down here for over a hundred years. That's my brother you're holding. Let him go."

"Not so fast," BB said. "Can you help us get back to the surface?"

"Hah! Do you know how far down we are? Getting to the surface will take days. Some creatures will help you, but others want to kill you.

And if we come with you they'll kill us too. We're tall and fast and we can blend in. But we don't have any weapons. That's why we live here where no one else lives. We're safe here—most of the time. Now let him go."

"Okay," BB said. "But only if you agree to take us to your leader. We've got to get out of here."

"Follow us."

Jepson and the other Clamp began slowly walking through the dark tunnel. The gang followed closely behind with the third Clamp still tied up.

They walked and walked for what felt like miles. They crossed a small stream and entered a huge cave filled with small buildings, paths and lanterns. When the gang entered, they saw hundreds of Clamps. They all stopped what they were doing and stared at the boys. Some of them were trying to blend into the cave walls like fossils.

Jepson led them straight toward an old building. It looked like it was built out of sticks and cardboard.

A green Clamp sat inside at a large table. He frowned as the boys walked in.

"My father—Diddy," Jepson said as he pointed to the green Clamp. "He's our leader. You got what you wanted. Now let my brother go!"

Kerry untied the belt and Jepson's brother immediately backed away from them.

Jepson explained everything to his father, who told the boys to sit down. They each took a seat at the table.

"Why did you want to see me?" Diddy asked.

"We thought you might be able to help us get out of here," BB said.

"What's your name?"

"Silas. But my friends call me BB."

"BB, have you ever seen a Clamp before?" Diddy asked, looking at the boys curiously.

The boys shook their heads.

"Do you trust us?"

The boys nodded.

"Are you sure that's a good idea?" Diddy asked.

The boys looked at each other. Jepson walked over and closed the big door they had just come through. The only light in the room came from the toothpicks on their heads.

CHAPTER 6

BUILDING BRIDGES

The boys squirmed nervously as they sat at the table.

"Some Clamps won't like that we're helping you," Diddy said. "Outsiders can be dangerous."

Jepson lit the lanterns around the room. The bright lights surrounded the room with a warm, comforting glow.

Diddy's face softened. "You need to be careful in these tunnels. We don't want to hurt you, but others will."

"We don't know much about other territories," Jepson explained.

Diddy nodded. "After you cross the river that borders our land, you'll be on your own again. Our historians tell us that's the land of the Angelicas. They're kind. They'll help you. But beware of the Strikers. They invaded that area years ago. They've been terrorizing the Angelicas ever since."

"Strikers are pure evil," Jepson said. "They kill each other and they don't treat anyone else any better."

Diddy added, "The only thing that saves us from them is that they can't swim."

Jepson leaned toward the boys. "See these two small slits I have behind each of my ears?"

"Yes," Pete said. "What are those for?"

"They allow us to breathe underwater. We can live underwater for days. That really makes the Strikers mad."

Diddy went on to explain the history of the Clamps and how they came to live in their cave.

He pointed to his green skin. "You can tell how old a Clamp is by the color of their skin. I'm green because I'm very old. Jepson is yellow because he has much more to learn from life."

Cliff's stomach growled loudly. "What do Clamps eat?" he asked.

"We'll show you."

Diddy and Jepson led the boys to another small cave that was filled with trees. Their branches were covered with fruit that looked like black apples. Diddy handed one to each boy.

"Mmm," Toby said, taking a bite. "These are great!"

As they ate, Diddy told them all about the tunnels.

"I learned everything about life in the tunnels from my grandfather. He explored them before they became as dangerous as they are now. During my lifetime I've only seen a few tunnels. But there are hundreds and hundreds of them."

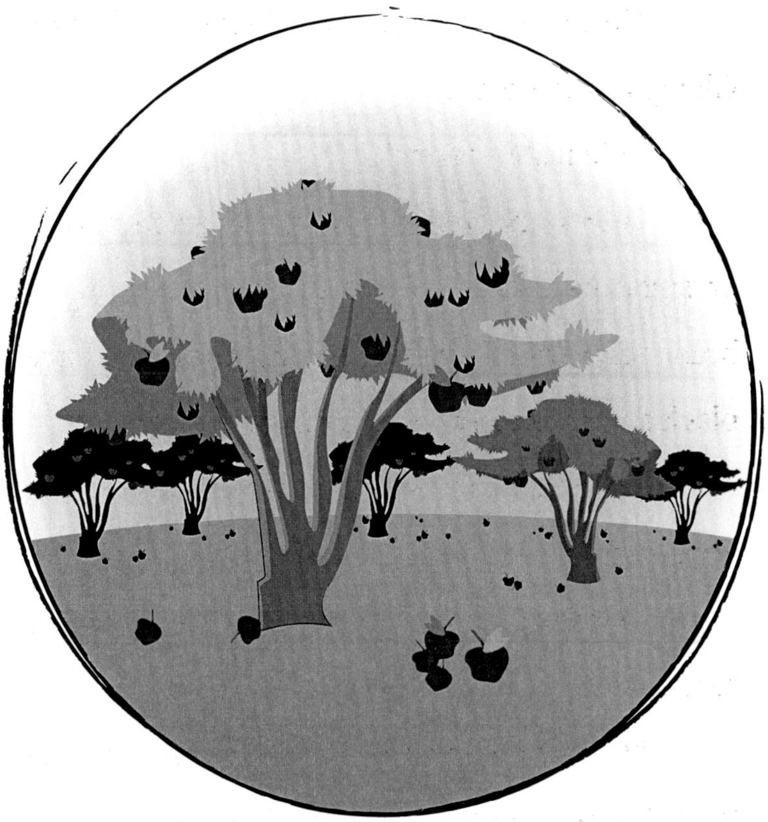

"We know it's dangerous, but we've got to get out of here," BB explained. "We'll stick together and fight off anything that tries to stop us."

"Thanks for everything," the boys told Diddy and Jepson as they began to gather their things to leave.

Just as the gang was about to leave, another Clamp frantically ran up to Diddy.

"Snardley!" Diddy exclaimed. "What's wrong?"

"There's been a cave-in! Smoker and Speedy were checking out the area where the bridge collapsed. They were trying to figure out a new way to get to our farm across the bridge. But part of the tunnel fell down and trapped them!"

"Are they alive?" Diddy asked.

"We can't tell. We've been trying to tap on the rocks, but I don't think they can hear us."

"Then we'll have to assume they're still alive," Diddy said. "Let's send in our rescue team."

Snardley sped off to gather the team.

The gang looked around at each other. "Is that the bridge our bus crashed down on?" Toby asked.

"Yes," Diddy answered. "Your bus fell through that sink hole and took out our most important bridge. Although it's at the far end of our territory, it connects our town with some of our best apple groves."

Jepson added, "We need to find a way to save those guys and get across to the other tunnel. It'll be hard for us to survive without the food we get from over there."

BB said, "Before we leave, I want to talk with the rest of the gang. Is there a place we can do that?"

"I'll show you where you can talk," Jepson said. "It's a building we made in honor of an unknown God. During times like this, when our friends' lives are at stake, we go there to talk to the great God who created everything."

Sammy asked, "What do you mean 'unknown God'?"

Diddy answered, "We don't know anything about this God. But we do believe that nothing around us—including us—got here by accident."

Once the gang was alone, BB said, "Guys, I want to go home as much as you all do. But I also want to help the Clamps. I just don't know what the right thing to do is."

"We've only been here a couple hours," Toby said. "But they've been really kind to us."

"And this problem they have is kind of our fault," John said. "I'd hate to see Smoker and Speedy hurt or killed because that bus crushed their bridge."

Kerry nodded. "It would be hard to just leave when they need help. We're stronger than they are. And we have our crowbar, pole and chain."

"I think we can spend one more day trying to help," Spencer said. "Giving something up to help someone else makes us tougher. I vote we ask Diddy if we can help!"

"Can we stand on the rock first?" Sammy asked.

"Sure!"

Sammy stepped on top. The rock groaned, then vibrated and a voice said,

"As I walked around, I looked carefully at the things you worship. I even found an altar with TO AN UNKNOWN GOD *written on it... Now I am going to tell you about this 'unknown god.' He is the God who made the world. He also made everything in it. He is the Lord of heaven and earth. He doesn't live in temples built by human hands."* [*]

---

[*] Acts 17:23-24

After the voice stopped, Sammy kept standing on the rock. He was deep in thought.

Suddenly it let out another loud groan. It vibrated a second time and then said,

"Give, and it will be given to you. A good amount will be poured into your lap. It will be pressed down, shaken together, and running over. The same amount you give will be measured out to you." *

"Sounds like it's telling us to help the Clamps," BB said.

"Yeah," Sammy agreed. "It also sounds like the unknown God Jepson talked about is the same God I've learned about in church."

"I don't really believe in God," Pete said. "But I'm okay with people who do. Either way I want to help the Clamps save their friends. I also want to figure out how to build a new bridge so they can get to their food supply."

---

*   Luke 6:38

"How would we do that?" John asked.

"I read a book about how they built the Golden Gate Bridge in San Francisco. I'm sure we could find some rope and wood that we could use."

"Good idea, Pete," BB said. "Does anyone have anything else to say?"

Everyone shook their heads no.

"Remember—we all agreed to stick together. All in favor of staying to help?"

"Aye!" the gang answered.

"I'll make sure that's okay with Diddy!" BB called as he ran out of the room.

After BB explained everything, Diddy said, "I'm surprised and honored that you want to help us. I know how badly you want to go home. In the past humans haven't always treated us very well. Your kindness will help to heal some of that pain."

"Can one of you take some of us to the cave-in so we can help dig out Smoker and Speedy?" BB asked. "And some of us would like to see what you have here to rebuild that bridge. Our friend Pete is really good at making things."

"We have a shack where we keep a lot of tools and different materials we've found over the years. The miners that abandoned these tunnels left a lot of supplies behind. They had to leave quickly because of all the cave-ins. So you can help us, but you need to be careful."

"How do you know if a tunnel is safe?" BB asked.

"Sometimes the ground shifts and you can see cracks or small rock slides. But most of the time there's no warning."

BB said, "That's what happened to us in the bus. We thought the ground was stable—but it wasn't."

"Silverfish!" Diddy called. A light green Clamp scurried over. "Can you take some of BB's team to the miner's shack? And tell Buggy to take the rest of them to the cave-in to help out."

BB followed Silverfish back to the rest of the gang. When they got there everyone decided that Pete, John, Spencer and Sammy would go to the miner's shed.

There they found old railroad ties and rails, ropes and nails. Pete took charge as they got to work.

"We need to make it sturdy enough to slide from one tunnel opening to the other," he explained. "We'll make it in sections. Then we'll be able to get it through some of the bends in the tunnel. We'll put it all together once we get to the drop-off."

Sammy used a rock to hammer a piece into place. "This bridge won't be perfect, but I think your plan will work, Pete."

"I wonder if Diddy knows how to get to any of the tunnels above here," Spencer said. "If they can't dig the Clamps out of the cave-in, maybe we can try to get to them from up above."

He grunted as he tried to lift a rail. "Can someone grab the other end of this rail? It's too heavy."

John came over to help. "If this plan works, it'll be worth it. I hope we can help some of the other creatures down here before we head home. It feels good to make someone else's life better if you can."

"Yeah," Spencer agreed. "It's boring to always think about yourself. There! I think we have the first two parts of the bridge done."

"Great!" Pete said. "Let's keep going. I think we're going to need 11 or 12 pieces. It's kind of hard to tell when we don't have a tape measure."

Meanwhile, the rest of the gang walked toward the cave-in.

"Could you slow down, Buggy?" BB asked. "You Clamps are really fast."

"And we're lugging all this stuff to use for digging!" Cliff added

"Sorry!" Buggy replied. "I'm just worried about my friends. I hope you can help us."

"We'll do our best," BB said. "We'll make a better plan once we get there."

As the gang approached, Snardley and the rescue team looked like they didn't make much progress. They stood looking at a big pile of rocks and dirt.

"How can we help?" BB asked.

"We're not strong enough to move some of these big rocks," Snardley told them.

"We could start an assembly line," Kerry suggested. "We'll move the rocks faster and farther that way."

Cliff stood on his tiptoes and peered over the mound. "There are some little holes along the top of the pile. I can try to dig through those with my hands. Smoker and Speedy might be able to see me. That way they'll know we're not giving up on them. It would give them some hope."

For the next hour, the gang worked alongside the Clamps. They used Toby's chain to move the bigger rocks. They pulled away dirt with their hands. Kerry's assembly line moved a bunch of smaller rocks to a nearby cave room.

Cliff climbed on top of the mound. After digging for a while he called out, "Smoker, can you hear me?"

"Yes," came the muffled reply. "Who are you?"

"I'm Cliff. My friends and I are helping to get you out. Are you okay?"

"We're fine! We've been standing on a ledge right next to the drop off."

Speedy added, "If any more dirt had fallen in, we would've been pushed off the ledge!"

"Hang in there!" Cliff said. "We're working hard to get this cleared out. We want you guys to walk out of here in one piece."

"We can start helping at our end!" Smoker said. "We'll throw rocks into the sinkhole. I don't think we have to worry about filling it up."

Cliff laughed. "I think that sinkhole would hold a whole mountain of dirt if we could carry it."

With renewed energy, both sides worked hard to clear a path through the mess. After a while the rest of the gang arrived with the bridge pieces.

"Do you think you guys are going to make it through?" Pete asked.

"We just talked to Smoker and Speedy," BB said. "They're helping on their side too. We should meet up with them soon!"

Cliff added, "Once we do that we'll have a big enough opening to get the bridge through."

"It'll be a miracle if you can get another bridge set up," Snardley said. "I don't know what we would do without our farmland."

Pretty soon the opening was clear enough that Smoker and Speedy could break free. Everyone cheered and hugged them both. After the celebration ended, they all kept working together to make enough room to get the sections of the bridge in place.

"Let's slide these sections together," Pete said. "Then we'll attach them to the tunnel floor."

Toby watched Pete arrange the bridge. "You did a great job, Pete! This bridge looks like it'll last for a long time."

Sammy hammered one last nail into the first piece of the bridge. Spencer pushed down on it with one foot.

"I think it'll hold my weight! Hand me the next piece and I'll attach it out here."

Cliff and Sammy hooked the chain around Spencer just in case. He crawled to the edge of the bridge and attached the next piece.

"I'm glad we made an extra piece," John said. "It looks like we'll need all of them. Are you still okay out there, Spencer?"

Spencer balanced himself on the edge of the bridge. "It feels just like I'm out on the high dive! Except I can't see the bottom of this huge hole. Hand me another section!"

"If some of you hold on to the end of this rope, I'll crawl out there to help Spencer," Kerry said.

"Thanks," Spencer said. "This is getting harder to do all by myself. Now I know what construction guys feel like when they're building those skyscrapers."

The Clamps were so excited to start using their new bridge. When it was finished, they ran back and forth across it. They laughed and hugged everyone again.

Sammy smiled as they walked back toward the village. "That felt good to help them out."

"Yeah," Kerry agreed. "But now that we're done, we have to leave the Clamps. And you know what that means..."

"Strikers!" Cliff whispered.

CHAPTER 7

A TIME TO FIGHT

The gang stood in front of Diddy for the last time.

"We have to go now," BB said. "And we want to leave you something. A piece of our rock fell off, and we think it should go in your chapel to the unknown God."

Sammy added, "Some of us think that listening to this rock's voice helps us understand God."

Diddy smiled. "You've saved my friends. You've helped us get our food supply back. And now you've given us something to help us in the future. Although humans have hurt us in the past, you've shown us they can do good too. We wish you well on your journey."

Jepson filled several small sacks with black apples and gave the boys some advice for surviving in the tunnels. They thanked him and said their goodbyes. Smoker and Speedy led them to a spot on the riverbank where it was shallow enough for them to cross.

"Thanks for saving our lives," Smoker said.

Speedy added, "Without that bridge a lot of us would've starved."

"Safe travels!" they called as they walked back to their village.

The boys were alone again.

Spencer stared into the water. "I wish we could've stayed with them longer."

"Me too," said Kerry.

The boys took off their shoes and socks. They rolled up their pant legs and began to trudge across the river. The water was cold. It stretched on for several miles.

Cliff and Toby held the chain and pole like weapons in case anything tried to attack them. Several hours had passed by the time they finally reached the other side.

"We made it," BB said, plopping down on the ground and stretching out his arms and legs. "The land of the Angelicas."

Spencer looked around. "The Angelicas sounded like they would be nice. I don't know why those mean old Strikers want to kill them."

"Yeah," Pete agreed. "If we run into anyone here I hope it's an Angelica. Maybe they'll help us."

"We've got to keep moving," BB said. "Diddy said it'll take us hours to get through this area."

"Cliff and I can go first," Toby offered. "I hope we don't run into any Strikers. But if we do, I can swing the chain and Cliff has the pole."

"I can go next," Kerry said as he held up the crowbar. "And John can come after me—he's got the hammer."

"Okay," BB said. "The rest of us can carry everything else. Are we missing anything?"

"Let's see if the rock has anything to say before we start," Sammy said. "Maybe it can tell us something that will help us."

Spencer put the rock on the ground and stepped on it. A loud groan echoed through the tunnel and it began to vibrate. It said,

"To you a thousand years are like a day that has just gone by. They are like a few hours of the night." *

"That sounds like something my dad taught about in church before," Sammy said. "He said God's time works differently than ours. I've been worried about people looking for us. Maybe time is different down here than it is in

---

* Psalm 90:4

our world. Our families might not even know we're missing yet."

"I was worried about that too," BB said. "But this is such a strange and magical place. It wouldn't feel very good to know all of our families were unhappy and worried while we're on this journey. Maybe they just think we're still fishing!"

"I wonder…" Sammy said as he looked at the rock.

He stepped on it a second time. After it groaned and vibrated, the voice said,

"Our fight is not against human beings. It is against the rulers, the authorities and the powers of this dark world. It is against the spiritual forces of evil in the heavenly world." *

"What's that supposed to mean?" Pete asked.

* Ephesians 6:12

"It means we probably won't be fighting other humans down here," John said.

"It said something about evil too," Sammy added. "My dad told me there's good and evil in the world and we have to choose between them."

"Why would anyone want to pick evil over good?" Kerry asked.

"I think evil can be really powerful," BB said. "We all think we're important, and we want things to go our way. Sometimes we do whatever we can to win. We don't care about hurting someone to get there."

"I learned in Sunday school that we all have an evil part inside of us," Sammy said. "Sometimes we do bad things and we forget about what it does to other people."

Toby nodded. "I feel like I'm always getting into trouble without trying to."

"This is kind of like what the rock said the other day," Cliff said. "About how sometimes we have to pay attention to things we can't see—like good and evil. We can't actually see good and evil, but we have to make sure we're not doing evil things. It's like the Strikers and Angelicas are fighting inside of me. And I have to make sure the Angelicas win."

"It seems like no matter what—we need to be ready to fight," Sammy said. "We have to fight against ourselves when we want to do bad things. And we have to look out for bad guys and fight them at the same time."

They boys sat in silence for a few minutes, thinking about these lessons.

Toby finally broke the silence. "Well, I'm ready to fight!" he said. He picked up the chain and started toward the next tunnel.

One by one the boys grabbed their belongings and followed Toby. They walked for what seemed like ages, eventually finding themselves at the entrance to a large cave. Suddenly something came flying toward Toby.

"Whoa!" he yelled, jumping back. A silver spear stuck in the ground between his feet.

"Get down!" he called.

More spears came zooming through the air. The gang dove behind several rocks.

"Where are they coming from?" Spencer asked.

Kerry pointed to a big boulder at the other end of the cave. "There—I think."

"That has to be Strikers," Cliff said. "I don't think Angelicas would just attack us like that."

"What do we do now?" John asked.

"Let's wait here for a little while," Cliff suggested. "We don't know how many there are. We can throw these smaller rocks at them if we need to."

"What if they come at us?" Sammy asked.

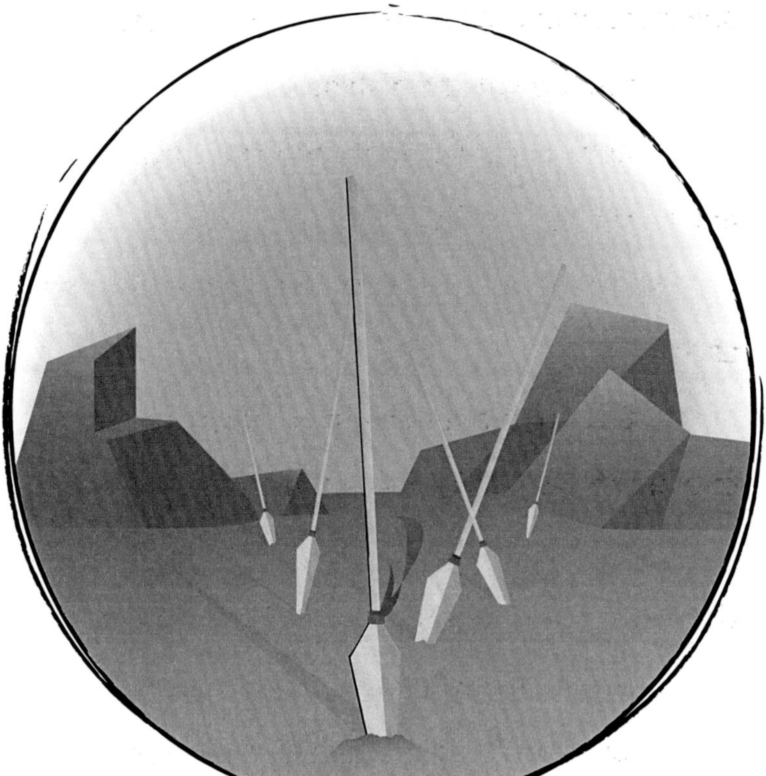

"Toby, Kerry and I have the best weapons," Cliff said. "So we can try to fight them off first. You guys follow behind us and throw the rocks at them."

"Look." Toby pointed at the spears sticking in the ground near them. "If we can get to those—we could use them too."

"There are six spears," Sammy pointed out. "Maybe that means there are six Strikers. So there are more of us than there are of them."

"I could crawl over there," Spencer offered, "and see if I can get a look at how many there are."

BB nodded. "Good idea. John, can you go with Spencer in case he needs help?"

"Sure!"

Spencer started army crawling toward the spears. He stopped behind a large boulder and peeked around it. John slowly followed behind him.

"Something's moving," Spencer whispered. "It looks like there are three of them over to the left. And three more are on our right."

"What do they look like?" Toby asked.

"Sort of like giant caterpillars. But they have sharp tooth-like things sticking out of their backs."

Spencer crawled forward some more. "They have two big arms too. And they're all holding more spears. Or maybe they're swords."

He stretched as far as he could and grabbed two spears before crawling back. "These guys look tough," he said.

"We need a plan to fight them off before they try to attack us again," BB said. "Let's split up. Three of you go to the right. Three go to the left. Pete and I will stay here so we can go where we're needed the most. Hoot if you need help. And when I say go—Sammy, what are you doing?"

Everyone turned toward Sammy as he stepped onto the rock.

"I thought this might help!" he whispered as it began to vibrate.

"Dear children, you belong to God. You have not accepted the teachings of the false prophets. That's because the one who is in you is powerful. He is more powerful than the one who is in the world." *

"My dad says that God is inside of me," Sammy said. "And that He's really strong. God will protect us, and He'll help us fight!"

"I sure hope so!" Cliff said.

"Here they come!" Spencer called. "Those things definitely aren't coming to say hi."

BB told everyone to go to their places. His voice echoed through the cave as he yelled "GO!"

Toby jumped out first with his chain swinging. He hit two Strikers at once. They squealed

---

* 1 John 4:4

and quickly wrapped their bodies around the chain, trying to dig their sharp teeth into it. Teeth shattered everywhere as soon as they bit down.

A third Striker lunged toward Toby. Just before its sword slammed into his legs, Kerry used his crowbar to knock it to the ground. John quickly dropped a rock on top of it. It kept wriggling—even under the weight of the rock.

Kerry hit it again with the crowbar, right on the back of its wide neck. It immediately stopped moving. John picked up the dead Striker's sword and ran to help Toby.

"These things are nasty!" Toby yelled. "They grabbed onto the chain and won't let go!"

While two of the Strikers struggled with Toby, John snuck up behind them. He hit one hard on the back of its neck with his sword. He hit the other in the same place. Both Strikers laid motionless on the ground.

Cliff peered over the top of his rock. The Striker closest to him was watching Toby and John's battle. Cliff jumped out to fight it as it started moving toward his friends.

"The neck!" he heard someone yell. "Hit him on the neck!"

Cliff swung the pole around and hit the Striker on the back of its neck. It fell to the ground and didn't move.

"Two to go!" he yelled.

He heard a loud hoot coming from the center of the cave.

Spencer and Sammy were throwing their rocks and spears at the rest of the Strikers. But they just seemed to be getting angrier and stronger.

Pete and BB moved in quickly to help. As the four boys threw rocks and tried to hit the remaining two Strikers with their spears, Toby snuck up behind them.

Wham! He hit one of them on the neck with the chain. *Wham!* He hit the second one.

When all six Strikers were lying still on the ground, the boys collapsed with relief. They wiped the sweat and dirt from their bodies and tried to catch their breath.

After a while John said, "If we have to do this again, we've got to go for their necks. It's their weakest part."

"And try to get them to wrap around something," Toby added. "Then they can't get you with their teeth. It was kind of fun watching them try to bite through that chain."

"Is everyone okay?" BB asked.

"Yeah!"

"I think the rock was right," Sammy said. "I feel like God helped us win."

"Maybe," Toby said. "I don't really know much about God. But either someone helped us or we got very lucky. Those Strikers weren't going easy on us."

"Sammy, can you thank God for us?" Kerry asked.

"Sure. But you could do it too. Praying is easy. Just act like you're talking to someone."

"All right." Kerry took a deep breath. "Thanks for helping us, God. I'm glad you were here. Amen."

As soon as Kerry finished, Spencer called out, "Look!" He pointed toward the big boulder across the cave.

"That's a really big Striker," Cliff said.

"And he's got *two* swords!" John ducked further behind the rock.

The Striker looked straight at the gang. "We'll be back!" he called. "Next time you'll be our prisoners!"

CHAPTER 8

CHOOSING YOUR OWN PATH

"Is he gone?" John whispered.

Spencer peeked out from behind the rock. "I think so."

"We should get out of here," BB said. "I don't want to be here when that Striker comes back."

The boys all got up and followed BB toward the next tunnel.

"We have to figure out a way to avoid him," John said. "This is such a maze of tunnels. If *we* can get lost in here, maybe we can lose him too."

"I just want to get home," Spencer said. "And I don't plan on asking a Striker how to get there. I think he has other plans for us…"

BB stopped short. The gang all looked up ahead. Right in front of them the tunnel split in two.

"Which way do we go *now*?" Cliff asked.

"We could flip a coin," Spencer suggested.

Sammy said, "Why don't we see what the rock has to say?"

He stepped on the rock. It groaned, then vibrated and a voice said,

> "Find delight in the Lord. Then he will give you everything your heart really wants." *

"What kind of answer is *that*?" John asked.

"I think it's telling us to be happy that God is with us," Sammy said.

---

*   Psalm 37:4

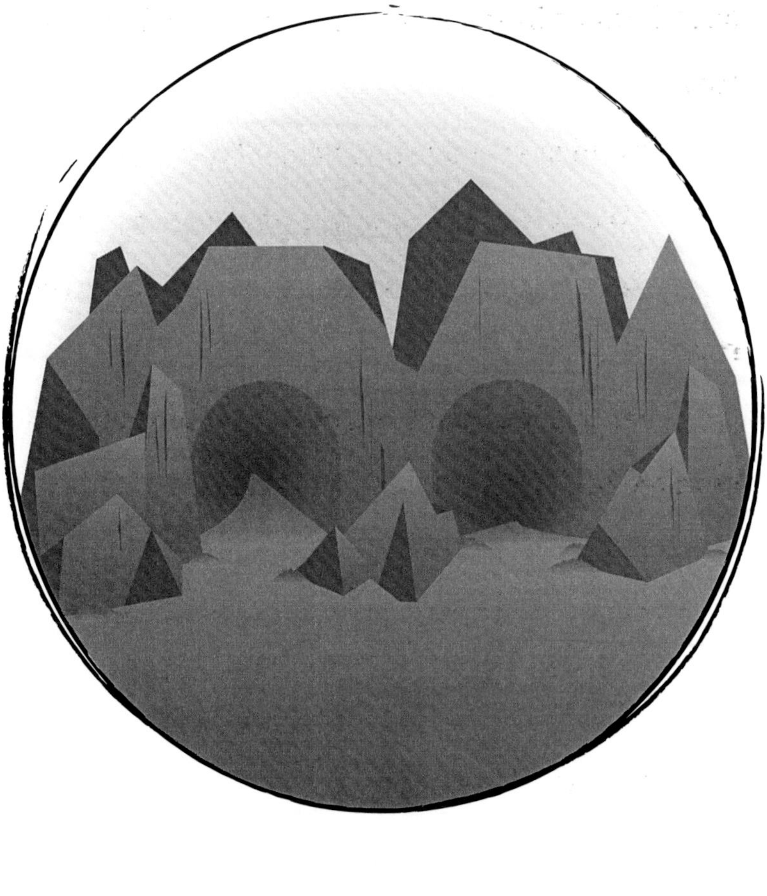

BB nodded. "Hmm. Well, it didn't tell us which tunnel to pick. Maybe that's because it doesn't matter which way we choose to go. What's important is that we keep moving forward and follow what the rock says."

"Well, whatever it means," John said, "we have to choose something."

Toby pointed to the tunnel on the left. "That one looks like it goes uphill, and the other one looks like it goes down. Maybe that doesn't mean anything... but if we want to go home, we have to go up."

"You're right," Cliff said.

"Who thinks we should take the uphill tunnel?" BB asked.

Everyone raised their hand.

After walking for a few minutes, the tunnel opened up into a massive cave room. It looked quite different from the caves they were used to seeing. The ground was flat, and it stretched on for miles. Golden grass covered every inch—for as far as they could see.

"Wow," Cliff said. "That's awesome."

"The grass—it feels just like I'm walking on carpet," Spencer added.

"Check that out," Toby said.

He was pointing at something far off in the distance. It looked like an old building with a shed behind it.

"There's a pond too," Cliff added. "And a creek going around that building."

"It's like a castle with a moat around it," John said.

"Well, that's good news," Spencer said. "If we can get to that building we'll be safe from the Strikers. They can't swim, remember?"

"You're right!" BB said. "Let's get over there. Quick!"

After crossing the creek, the gang decided to explore the area a little. When they had looked around for a while, BB called them all back together to see what everyone found.

Sammy said, "Spencer and I found some old metal cots that must've been left by the miners."

"I found some cans of beans and corn in the kitchen," Kerry said. "We could make a fire and cook them over that."

"We could try to catch some fish from the pond too," Pete added. "John and I found some fishing poles and lures in the shed."

"Speaking of campfires," Sammy said, "I found something interesting."

"What is it?" Toby asked.

"Between the shed and the house there's a fire pit filled with wood—ready to be lit. It looks like someone set it all up and then never used it."

"This sounds great!" Cliff said. "We can eat by the fire tonight, just like we do at home."

"There's something else over there too..." Sammy said. "Beside the fire pit there was a big, old book. It's filled with blank pages—just like Pops' book."

"No way," Cliff said in disbelief.

"It's true! C'mon, I'll show you."

Everyone followed Sammy to the fire pit. After flipping through the blank pages of the book, they decided to set it aside and started getting ready for dinner.

They caught five big trout and cooked them with the corn and beans. After they ate as much as they could, they all just sat there—tired and relaxed. They stared quietly into the roaring fire.

Each boy was deep in his own thoughts. In the stillness, they thought about this new part of life they had been discovering. They thought about the brave choices they had been making and how glad they were to have their friends beside them.

Suddenly Sammy broke the silence.

"Ouch!" he yelled.

"What's wrong?" BB asked.

"A little bird just flew past, and it clawed me!"

"That's weird," Cliff said, looking around. "I wonder where it came from."

Sammy ducked. "Here it comes again!"

"Stay still, Sammy," Toby said. "It looks like it's going to land on your shoulder!"

A small yellow bird hovered above Sammy.

"It might be tame," Toby continued. "My stepdad told me miners used to bring birds down into the mines. They used them to sense poisonous gas that people couldn't smell. Since they're so small, the birds would die from breathing the gas, but that gave the miners time to get out."

Pete said, "Well, that one is alive and well. And it looks like it likes Sammy."

"Maybe we should try to catch it and keep it as a pet," John suggested.

By this time the bird was sitting calmly on Sammy's right shoulder. Sammy sat as still as he could so he wouldn't scare it away.

The bird turned its head toward Sammy. It opened its beak.

"Tell him not to waste his time trying to catch me," the bird whispered. "I go where I go."

Sammy's eyes widened. He said to the gang, "I guess nothing down here can surprise you guys anymore... but this bird just talked to me."

"Well, tell him to speak up," Cliff said.

"I'll only talk to you," the bird chirped in Sammy's ear.

"What's your name?" Sammy asked.

"Some say I'm like the wind. So you can call me Wind."

Sammy continued to talk with Wind, telling the gang everything he said. They asked Sammy questions that he repeated to Wind.

"How long have you been here?"

"It seems like forever," Wind answered.

"Why are you talking to me?" Sammy asked.

"Because there are things you should know about the choices that you make."

"Does that mean you know how we can get home?"

Wind said, "There are several ways to get home. The question is what kind of boy would you like to be when you get there?"

"What do you mean?" Sammy asked.

"You can choose to play it safe," Wind explained. "That's what a lot of people do. They just take it easy and never try to learn what life can teach them. They don't become who they're meant to be. And they don't contribute much to the world."

"Oh." Sammy looked thoughtful. "Well, we're too young to contribute to the world, aren't we?"

"No, you're not," Wind chirped. "What about Smoker and Speedy? You saved their lives. That's huge!"

Sammy nodded. "You're right—we did. So what kind of choices will we have to make?"

"You're always making choices," Wind said. "Earlier you chose the tunnel that brought you here. Tomorrow you'll each choose whether to stay here or go back and take the other tunnel. Once you make that choice there'll be no turning back. There are times when you'll choose differently from each other. Sometimes everyone has to choose their *own* path."

"Do you know what'll happen if we decide to stay here?" Sammy asked.

"Someone will come to take care of you. If you decide to go back to the other tunnel, you'll face a series of tests. These tests will teach you many lessons. But you won't learn if you don't challenge yourself. It can be scary and exciting at the same time. Sometimes you'll fail. Sometimes you'll get hurt. But you'll also grow."

"Is it Pops that's coming to take care of us?" Sammy asked.

"Pops will always be there to help you wherever you go—even when you can't see him. You'll grow if you trust him and keep listening to the rock. So you can stay here and take it easy, or you can go on a journey that will make you stronger and bring you closer to your dreams. Now stand on the rock."

Sammy stood up, put the rock on the ground and stepped on top. The rock groaned, then vibrated and the voice said,

"So don't be afraid. You are worth more than many sparrows." *

---

*   Matthew 10:31

"If you choose to leave here," Wind continued, "you'll travel through a lot of different worlds. But each one will give you the chance to grow. You won't have these opportunities if you stay here."

When Wind had finished talking, he flew away.

"What else did he say?" Toby asked.

Cliff said, "You said something about a choice."

Sammy nodded. "Wind said we each have to make a choice about where we want to go from here. Whatever choice we make—there's no turning back. If we decide to stay here, eventually help will arrive. Or we can go back and take the other tunnel."

"I could handle a lot of nights like tonight," Pete said. "I think we should stay!"

"Wind said something else too," Sammy said. "If we take the other tunnel, it'll change us in a good way—and it'll make us stronger. We'll learn more lessons just like we've already been learning."

"That does sound more exciting than staying here," Toby said. "You know I love a good adventure. Yeah—it's been scary sometimes. But we've always gotten through it. If we stay here I think it'll get boring eventually."

"And we all heard what the rock said," BB pointed out. "We shouldn't be afraid—God will take care of us!"

"This is a pretty nice place," Kerry said. "I think it'll be hard to leave. Especially because we don't know what we're getting into. I don't always get Pops' lessons. But they always seem to make my life better when I try to follow them. So I'm ready to take the other tunnel. Bring it on!"

Cliff said, "We might run into some Strikers... but if that happens, I don't want you guys having all that fun without me."

"So we can stay here and wait for someone to come and help us," BB said. "Or we can go see what happens in the other tunnel. Along the way we can learn some lessons and keep getting stronger. Right, Sammy?"

Sammy nodded.

"Then let's vote!"

"I vote to go back to the other tunnel," Cliff said. "I've got to grow up sometime, and this adventure sounds like it'll make that happen!"

"I want to get stronger too," Toby agreed. "I might regret this later, but I have to see if I have enough in me to make it through that other tunnel."

"I liked helping the Clamps," Pete said. "Maybe we'll be able to do something like that again. But I don't think that'll happen if we just sit here taking it easy. So I'm for the other tunnel too!"

"Me too," John agreed.

"I trust Pops and the rock," Spencer said. "Every day I see the light from Pops' toothpicks and feel like he's right here with me. This plan feels risky—but let's do it!"

Kerry's eyes twinkled. "It *is* nice here. But really—what would life be like without Strikers?"

Sammy said, "I'm with you guys—let's go see what's in that other tunnel."

BB smiled. "I wouldn't be a very good leader if you all went one way and I decided to go the other way. You know I love Pops' lessons. It's like school—if we don't keep reading, we won't get smarter. So let's get some rest for now and head out on our next adventure tomorrow. I have a feeling that once we cross that creek and head down that other path, we're in for some real big surprises."

Sammy stood up in front of the gang. "All in favor of learning some more lessons?" he called.

A loud "Aye!" echoed through the valley.

coming up in
THE CAMPFIRE GANG
. . .

Sammy stepped on top of the rock. It groaned, then vibrated and then a voice said,

*"But those who trust in the L*ORD *will receive new strength. They will fly as high as eagles. They will run and not get tired. They will walk and not grow weak."* *

"What does that mean?" Kerry asked.

"I think it means God will help us fight hard," Spencer said.

"That gives me an idea…" Thaddeus said.

He called over eight Angelicas. He gave them some instructions and they started flying

---
* Isaiah 40:31

back toward their home.

The boys became more and more nervous as the sound of marching Strikers got louder and louder.

The group of Angelicas soon returned to the cave room. They were each holding some kind of thin, white fabric.

"Try these on," Thaddeus said as he gave one to each boy.

"They look like wings!" BB said.

Thaddeus nodded. "We make these for Angelicas who get hurt during our battles. But they might fit you too. Quick—try them on. Start practicing—maybe you'll be able to fly just like we can."

"Are you sure we can learn how to steer these things this quickly?" Toby asked nervously.

"I think you'll be safer trying to fly than staying on the ground. You'll learn fast because God will help you."

As soon as the words came out of his mouth, Strikers began pouring into the cave room.

BB looked at the gang. "Okay, guys—fight like this could be our last battle. Let's do our best!"

The boys courageously strapped on their new wings. Together they flew straight toward the mob of attacking Strikers.

order Book #2 at
www.TheCampfireGang.com